ISBN 0-9728654-0-3
Library of Congress Control Number: 2003090513
Diederich, Ellen Jean
Where's Petunia?

10 9 8 7 6 5 4 3 2 1
SAN: 2 5 5 - 1 5 2 7
Printed in Fargo, North Dakota, USA
Book Design by Sheyna Laurich

View other work by Ellen Jean Diederich at www.givinity.com

Giving Divine Images to You

Where's Petunia?

Written and Illustrated by Ellen Jean Diederich
Text Edited by Dr. Lynette L. Wert

Art

Petunia

DEDICATION & ACKNOWLEDGMENT:
To Monica & Brittany, my inspiration
and cat photographers,
Paul, Warren, & Irene, my sponsors,
Mom & Dad for always supporting me as an artist,
Lynette for her patient guidance.

Ellen Jean Diederich

When the vase of flowers crashed to the floor with a crunch, smash, crackle, I knew my tail had gotten me in trouble again. Beautiful blooms, water, and broken glass hit the rug, bounced on the piano keys, and dribbled all the way to the front door. Cats aren't as graceful as some humans claim we are. My pesky tail gets curious and excited ahead of the rest of me.

My name's Art. I'm the cat who owns the girls, Monica and Brittany, who live in our house. The other cat who lives here, Petunia, believes the humans own her. There's Petunia sitting on the windowsill. She's beautiful with her gray, white, and brown face and socks of different colors. Our favorite game is hide and seek outdoors. It's my turn to hide today.

Whoa, here comes our human with the broom. Of course, she bawled me out—not Petunia. "Oh, Art, what have you done now?" She opened the door to sweep out the mess. Petunia leaped off the windowsill and made a dash to the flower garden. I was stuck inside, miserable, listening to my lecture, and knowing Petunia would get first chance to hide now.

I heard my girls thumping down the stairs. They wear clompy flip-flop sandals so I always know where they are. Monica grabbed me and squeezed my middle. "In trouble again, Arty?" I gave a nervous purr to show I was sorry and tried to wiggle away.

Brittany was looking for Petunia. "Where's your buddy?" she asked me. I was anxious to escape the crime scene, so I performed my twist and stretch maneuver. Monica dropped me, and I hopped over the broken flower stems. 'Petunia is outside,' I meowed, putting a paw on the door. The girls took the hint. I made a mad dash for the porch before the wildly swinging screen door could trap my tail.

I love being outside. Some humans refer to Petunia and me as house cats, but it's not true. Sniffing the fresh air and frisking in the flower garden is my idea of a perfect day. I jumped on top of a wrought-iron garden chair and straightened my fur. I was keeping an eye out for Petunia, too. She's excellent at hiding.

These **hydrangeas** are beautiful—they look like balls of colored confetti. When Petunia curls up to sleep, she looks like a ball, too. Don't tell Petunia, but I know she likes me. Here's another secret: when we play hide and seek, she always hides in the flowers. She blends right in with the leaves and stems and patterns of color and sunshine.

There's Monica and Brittany ahead on the path by the **strawflowers**. "These flowers seem to be dancing," said Monica. "Don't they look like tiny ballerinas wearing tutus?"

Brittany was more interested in finding our cat-in-hiding. "The **strawflowers** are pretty," she answered, "But where's Petunia?"

The three of us trooped toward the chicken coop. No sign of Petunia so far. The hen house door was open today and the chickens were chit-chatting loudly. I heard them discussing the ribbons Monica and Brittany had used to decorate the coop.

Behind the coop I found several of my chicken friends scratching among flowers which have pink and orange blossoms and tiny yellow centers. I asked a tall rooster whose head stood up above the blooms, "Have you seen Petunia?"

He tilted his comb and crowed loudly, "Urr-uhh-urr! These are not Petunias. They are **begonias**."

eyond the wooden gate
would be a good hiding place,
I realized, so I peered through.
No Petunia. All I saw was
Monica and Brittany by the **zinnias**.
Brittany showed a flower to her
sister and said, "Look how high
the center perches on top.
The **zinnias** look like they
are wearing miniature crowns."

When I was surprised
by the cows, I jumped
with all four feet in the air
and did a somersault.
The cows looked huge,
standing neck deep in giant
pink and white flowers.
I put my feet back under me
and got my tail under control.
"Have you seen Petunia?"

"Don't be silly,"
mooed the lead cow.
"Can't you see these are
hollyhocks, not Petunias?"

This hide and seek game was turning into work. Petunia had such a head start, she must have found an excellent hiding place today. I followed my girls up the garden path.

When I tippy-toed into a purple flower patch, I noticed pointed green leaves and blossoms that had grown bloom-beards. More cows lounged nearby, so I asked, "Is Petunia here?"

The cows answered together, "No Petunias here! These are **irises**."

'Boy, oh boy,' I thought. 'Cows sure know their flowers!'

The sheep were standing watch quietly in tall, spiky flowers. The blossoms made hats and necklaces for the animals and seemed woven into their fluffy wool.

"I'm looking for Petunia," I purred.

The sheep raised their heads and looked side to side. "Not a Petunia in sight," said a ewe. "All these flowers are **salvia**."

Horses were whinnying but I couldn't see them.
I raced across the field toward the sound and
discovered the horses almost hidden by enormous
golden flowers. The petals were way above my head.
I arched my back and stood on my hind legs to meow,
"Anyone seen Petunia?"

One horse lowered his head and shook his mane
to say 'No.' He snorted, "Don't you know Petunias
are much, much shorter than these **sunflowers**?"

eighbor girls had come to play with Brittany and Monica. I listened as they recited nursery rhymes and made-up games in a patch of blooming **cleome**.

But perhaps I'd better move on. The last time these friends were here, they tried to make me wear boots. I swooshed down low and kept my tail quiet to make a silent getaway.

Pigs are smart—I'll check with them. By the pen, I discovered the pigs enjoying a wallow in a pile of freshly-cut **peonies**. "Is Petunia here?"

A pig raised his snout. "Use your nose, Art. Petunias don't smell half as good as **peonies**."

I didn't care to hear snooty insults about my friend, Petunia. Pigs are no help.

Whisking around the corner, I startled a rabbit nibbling **pansies**. My job is to shoo bunnies and other pests away. Standing tall, I growled to signal my attack. The rabbit flinched, put his ears up, and the chase was on. If only my humans would appreciate how hard I work and pay less attention to my troublesome tail.

The rabbit rounded the corner. I was close
behind. We ran straight into a flock of ducks.
They flapped and squawked and waddled
like frantic white wind-up toys into
the **snapdragons**.

That rabbit could really run, but
I was gaining on him. We raced
toward a gaggle of geese.
They saw us coming and
began honking loudly, then
scattered. Most of the geese
dived into the thick **delphiniums**.
As we zipped past, I heard
them scolding us in a
high-pitched chorus.
If I have to keep up this
chase, I'll never find Petunia.

The rabbit turned left, zooming toward the **lily** garden. Oh, no! Goats are munching there, too. All uninvited guests must scram! Ready...set...I gave my loudest 'MEEOOOWW!' while leaping toward the wheelbarrow. I felt my tail fur flying above my back like a propeller.

Goats scrambled lickety-split in all directions. They bleated loudly, dumped the wheelbarrow of **petunias** upside down, and trampled the **lilies**.

Another ruckus I'll get blamed for, I thought. Suddenly, from beneath the overturned wheelbarrow, I heard soft, scared mewing. My strong paws untangled the plants. There, with dirt and a funny look on her pretty face, was my Petunia. "I found you!" I teased. "What a clever idea, hiding a Petunia in the **petunias**."

"But Arty, I was only taking a nap in the wheelbarrow." She shook dust off her fur and licked around her whiskers, primping. "What happened?"

I explained briefly how I'd saved the gardens from intruders. "No way will I let goats and rabbits eat the flowers and mess up your hiding places," I assured her. Petunia ducked her head and smiled like she was proud of me. "But it was my turn to hide first today," I reminded her.

All the moos, quacks, honks, bleats, snorts, and meows brought Monica, Brittany, and the friends running to the yard. "This mess is from leaving the gate open," lectured Monica.

"Oops!" cried the playmates. "Sorry."

It's nice hearing someone else apologize. Brittany ordered everyone to close gates and help herd animals back to the pens, coops, and meadows. Then the girls collected the crumpled flowers and used buckets to line the sidewalk with slightly wilted bouquets.

I whispered to Petunia. "Let's go back to the house. I'm too tired to hide right now." We took the shortcut through the **sweet pea** vines. My bothersome tail hooked on one of the vines. I struggled until the whole flower bed rustled and shook, and I was wrapped head to toe.

"Aha!" cried Monica and Brittany together. "Our cats!"

onica stepped into the flowers and started unraveling the **sweet pea** vine that had trapped me. "Aren't they the cutest couple?" she asked her friends. She wound the **sweet pea** vines around Petunia's head and shoulders. "Oh look, it seems like Petunia's wearing a veil. Hey, let's pretend Art and Petunia are getting married!"

The girls giggled. Petunia pranced down the sidewalk between the buckets of flowers. The **sweet pea** veil trailed along.

Wedding?
What are these humans thinking!
A cat wedding is a purr-fectly awful idea. Being stuffed in boots was bad enough.
I'm not standing still for a tux and tails. I pounced on Petunia's silly veil and whispered,
"Catch you later for more hide and seek. Right now, consider me out of here!"

With a sideways leap, I escaped to peace and quiet. I'm headed to a secret spot for my
well-deserved cat nap. But tomorrow, I'll be up early and hide first.

begonia
bǐ gōn′yə

hydrangea
hī drān′jə

peony
pē′ə nē

strawflower
strô′ flou′ ər

Art

cleome
klē ō′ mē

iris
ī′rǐs

petunia
pǐ tōōn′yə

sunflower
sŭn′ flou′ ər

Petunia

delphinium
dĕl fǐn′ē əm

lily
lǐl′ē

salvia
săl′ vē ə

sweet pea
swēēt′ pē′

Monica

hollyhock
hŏl′ ē hŏk

pansy
păn′ zē

snapdragon
snăp′ drăg ən

zinnia
zǐn′ē ə

Brittany

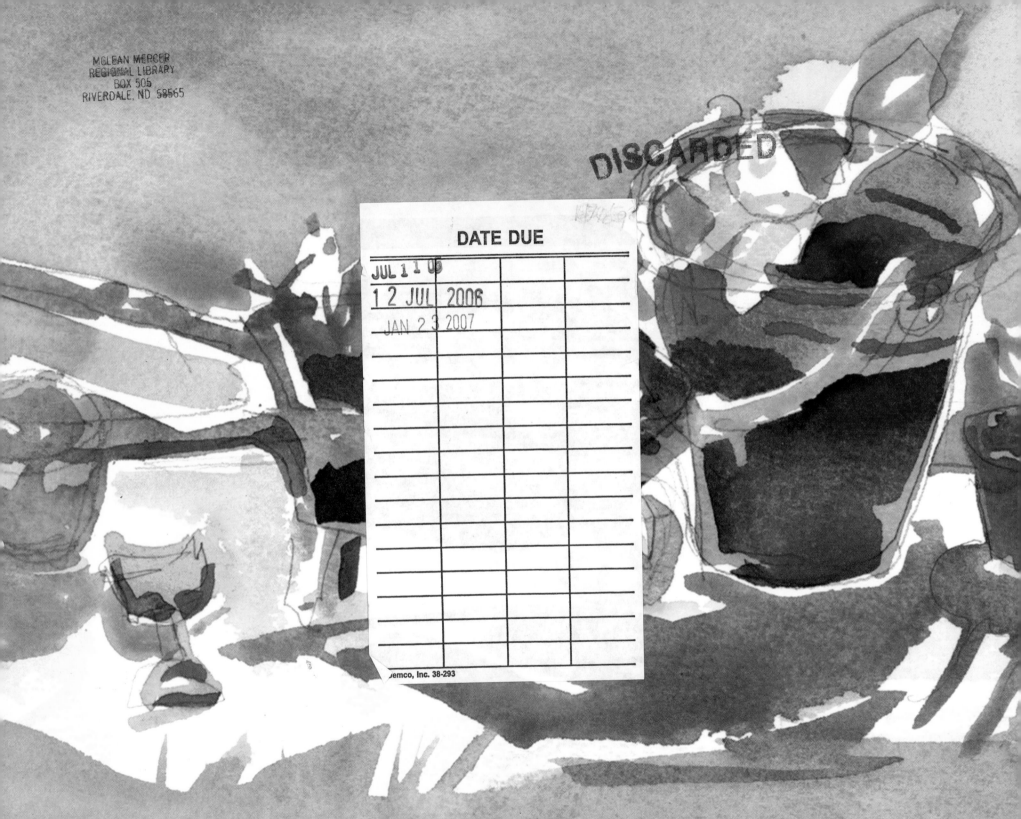

DATE DUE

JUL 1 1 05		
1 2 JUL 2006		
JAN 2 3 2007		

Demco, Inc. 38-293